DAVID
and the Seagulls

by Marion Downer

Illustrations by Victoria Skakandi

based on original photography by Yolla Niclas

Cover design by Tina DeKam

Originally published in 1956

This unabridged version has updated grammar and spelling.

© 2019 Jenny Phillips

goodandbeautiful.com

SEAL LEDGES
MONHEGAN ISLAND
SCHOOL
CALF COVE
SQUEAKER COVE
Monhegan Light House
SWIM BEACH
Fish BEACH
The MEADOW
MARKET
CHURCH
N
0 25 m

CHAPTER 1

Morning on Monhegan Island

Morning on Monhegan Island is no time to sleep. A wide-awake seagull waited on David Boynton's roof.

"Get up, boy," he seemed to say, but David was not asleep. He was up and away.

It was the first day of his summer vacation. Oh, he was glad to be back on the island! And he was glad he was old enough this year to have his father's old boat for his own.

David rowed a short distance out into the ocean for a good look at old Monhegan

Island and to see the white gulls flutter their wings and drift over the water.

A flock of seagulls soared above the boat. They were all alike—but not quite, to David. There was one he thought he had seen before. Could it be that seagull friend of his, the one he had kept in his yard last year?

He called to it, and the gull turned. It left the flock and flew straight down by David.

That was its way of saying, "Ho, David! Friendships are not forgotten."

Then David came ashore to look up old island friends. At Lobster Cove, he saw a painter he knew. The man took a moment to say, "Hello there, boy! Back again?"

Then he went on painting his picture of the sky, the ocean, and the beach grass—all in Monhegan's special colors.

David roamed over to Fisherman's Beach and sat down on a broad, storm-worn rock. He felt at home everywhere on the island, as if he had never been away.

And everyone looked friendly, even a dog

that ambled ahead of the busy fishermen.

David enjoyed the warm sun and listened to the cheerful talk of the hard-working fishermen.

After a while, David walked on.

He walked away from the low, pebbly shore and went to the highest place of all—the lighthouse hill. There the keeper of the light, as a special favor to David, took him up the winding stairs to the lighthouse top.

Near the lamp, David came through a door to look down at the island's curving edges and over miles of blue sea.

How the clouds rolled by! How far away everything was!

After a while, David wandered down the shore of a cove. Here he found things to look at closely. Flat on a stretch of sand lay a starfish. Its points looked like arms and legs covered with kernels of popcorn. At the waistline, the bumps formed a round belt buckle.

In the sand near the starfish were tracks leading to the water's edge.

David followed them.

There, in a crevice of the rock, a seagull had let itself slump down.

It looked forlorn and weak. David couldn't leave it there to die. Slowly and carefully, he picked up the limp body. He noticed that the feathers had the tawny colors always seen on gulls in their first year.

Although the gull was young and wild, it did not stir even when David held it close. He carried it through the forest and down a path to the other edge of the island—home.

Chapter 2
Smokey

The trip to David's house had been like an ambulance ride. And the pen in David's backyard had the comforts of a hospital—at least for birds. It had shelter, a straw bed, and a water basin.

The gull patient was not sick, not wounded, no bones were broken. Perhaps he was just hungry. Probably when fish had become scarce there, the older birds had deserted the cove, leaving this young one behind.

David fed the half-starved gull and named him Smokey.

Food and rest made Smokey's legs stand, but his wings stayed folded.

On those young wings, David knew, the gull had made its first flights not long before. And he knew where it had been hatched—offshore on a certain pile of rocks, the nesting place of all Monhegan seagulls, not too far from his home.

The nesting place of the gulls could be clearly seen from the shore of Monhegan. It was a bleak, sea-washed pile of rocks and had been named Nigh Duck by the first colonists.

David wondered what there was to see now at Nigh Duck and decided to take a visit in a boat to explore the hatching place of his gull, Smokey.

He ran his boat out to it.

Climbing over the rocks, he found a nest and two eggs.

The mother bird must have left to get food for herself and to exercise awhile.

The straws of the nest were wiry, but they had been laid in a circular way to fit into a chink in the weather-scarred boulders. The mother's feathers would shelter the eggs from the wind and cold salt spray.

And there at Nigh Duck, David saw a nest where eggs were hatching.

As he watched, he could hear the shells chipping. He could see two little bills tapping, tapping, hard at work to give two tiny creatures their first breaths of open air.

Then one chick came out. It had spots just like the spots on the shells.

Every gull chick's first ambition is to try its legs.

The ones David was watching walked around as soon as their downy coats had dried.

What if some enemy bird should swoop down and grab one of them, padding around on its little webbed feet?

Then David remembered that the spotted down and the speckled feathers would hide them from their enemies. Birds of prey would be fooled because the coloring and design looked so like the rough and creviced rocks.

Most baby gulls on Nigh Duck lived and grew up happily.

But David saw one chick that had tried its legs and lost its mother. He knew that very young gulls cannot feed themselves.

He kept watch over this one until he felt sure that no parent birds would come to poke food into its beak.

And out on a bare flat rock was another unfed chick. That made two who would starve if left alone. David picked them both up and warmed them in his hands, then put them in his boat and sped for home.

The poor chicks looked very frail and shaky when he lifted them out. He wondered if they would live.

CHAPTER 3
Nursing Two Chicks

When the chicks were in the pen, David cut some fish into bite-size pieces. He poked the food into the two little beaks just as a mother bird would do.

He poured fresh water into the basin and fixed a covered box for a bed.

Weeks passed. The baby gulls appeared to be happy and contented. David imagined he could see smiles on their faces. He was careful never to frighten the chicks, and he was very gentle when he held them and stroked their soft feathers. They knew he was their friend.

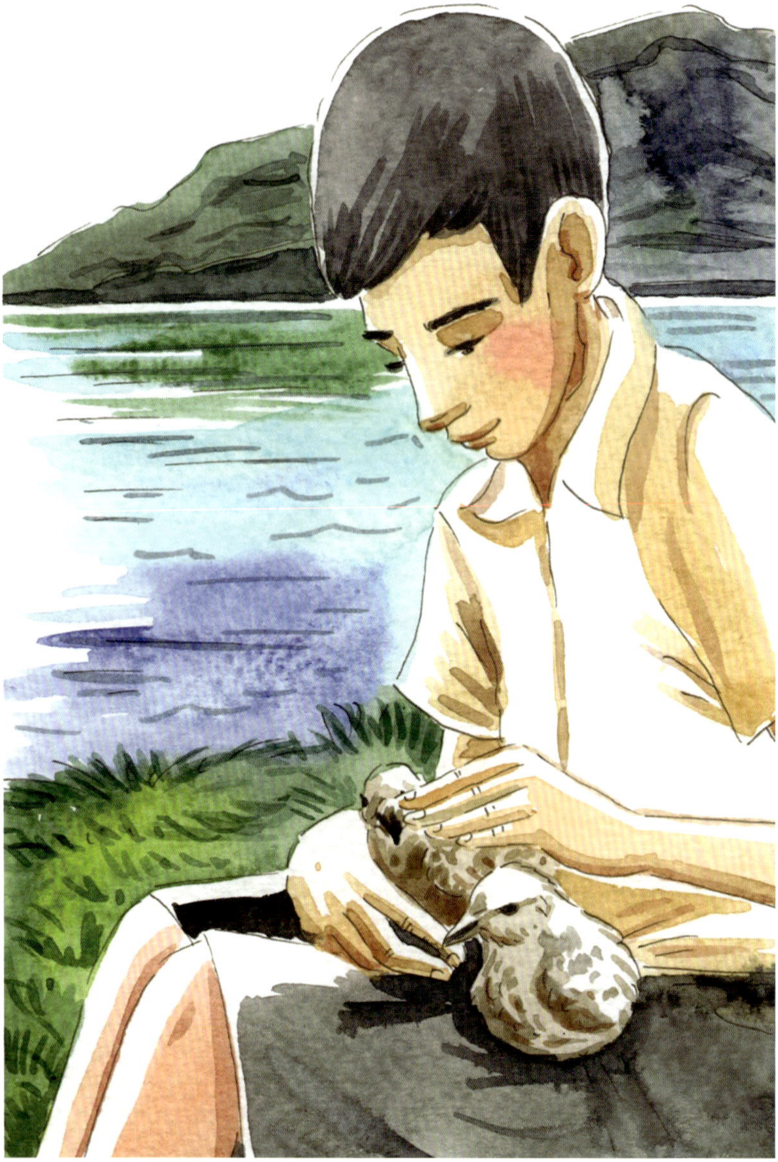

Standing on a ledge at the back of the house, they looked as funny as two little clowns with their spotted faces and their spreading feet. They cawed noisily to David, and he named them the "Squawks."

It was fun to care for the little Squawks, to keep them safe and watch them grow. But now the once-starved Smokey was so well and so happy that he liked to romp.

David told him to fly away. And fly away he did, quite often. But he always came back. The pen was home to Smokey.

Smokey was free to go, but he was still too young to keep up with the flocks of mature gulls that soared over the shores each day.

These white-feathered gulls would drift almost motionless on currents of wind, then arch their wings suddenly and turn back to make the same drift again.

They reminded David of skiers descending over and over some favorite hill.

In a sudden storm, one of the large white gulls made a wrong turn and fell. A man who saw it called David to come quickly.

"A disabled gull," he said, "out on the rocks!"

David hurried.

The waves roared, and he could hardly hear the man's voice as he motioned toward a point below the cliffs.

The gull was hard to see in the spray and the foam. At last David found the gull. It could not take off or even stand.

And it was beautiful—like an eagle.

One wing was useless. The other kept beating up and down in a frenzy of fear and pain. The fierce beak dared anyone to approach.

David moved nearer. He knew how to gain the confidence of a gull. Although this fierce one bit him on the nose, they came home together.

The gull had a broken wing and an injured leg. He would do no more soaring on the breeze or drifting on the ocean.

He was grounded! And in a pen! But his disposition was good, considering his troubles. David gave him an important sounding name—Orley.

Orley often stood looking on at the antics of his little pen-mates, the Squawks. The basin where they waded was far too small for a big gull.

David thought of a place to take Orley where he could have a swimming hole more suited to his size.

One day David carried Orley to a low place near the shore where water always remained when the tide went out. It was warmed by the sun and sheltered from wind by rocks.

David watched anxiously. How would Orley manage, even in this quiet pool, with his ailing leg and his drooping wing? He need not have worried.

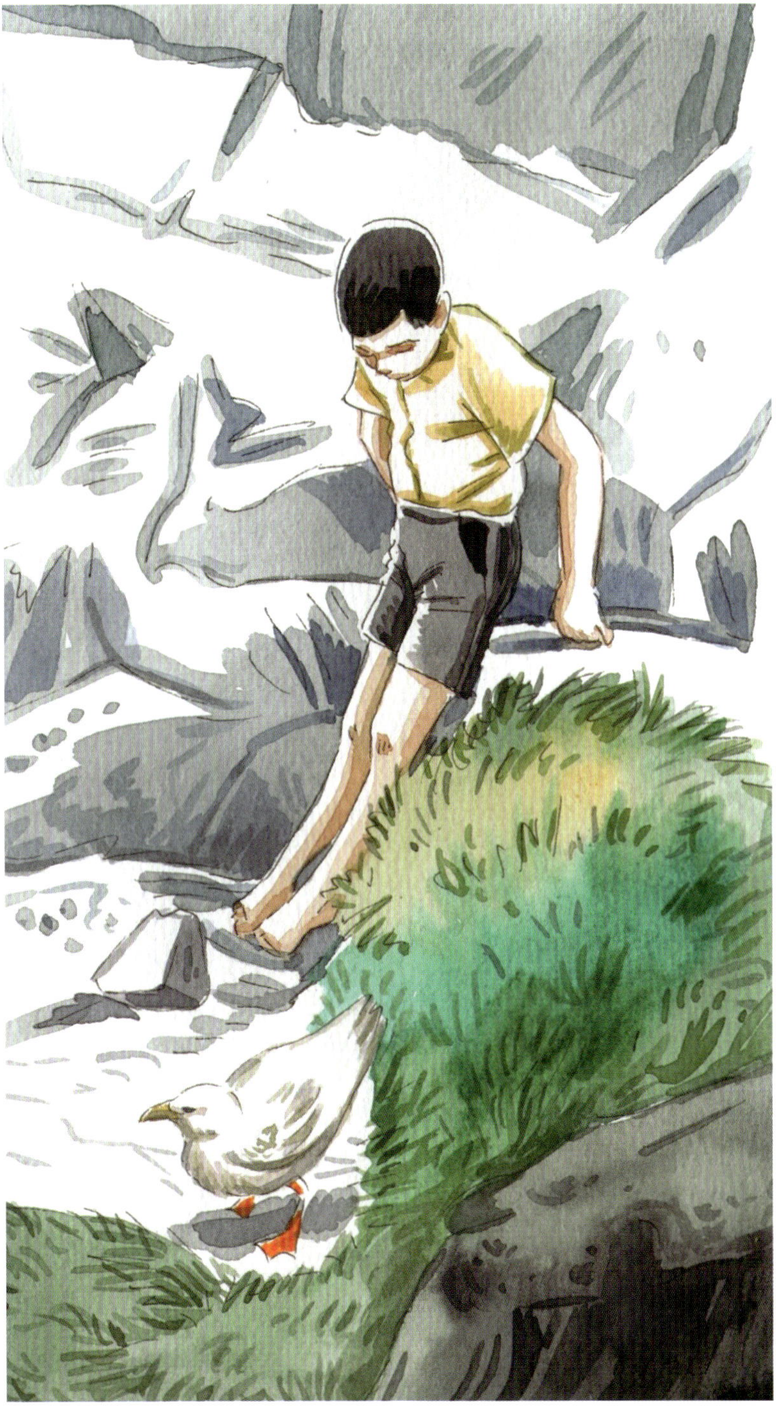

The tide pool suited Orley so well that soon the bird was leading the way there and letting the boy follow.

The leg had healed, and though the wing still dragged, Orley bobbed along over the rough ground and down a jagged cliff in the very best of spirits.

He made sure that David was not far behind. He always seemed to understand what was being done for him.

Orley was all right, but now those growing Squawks were a problem. They must learn to fly, and they had no parents to teach them, so David would have to do it.

David had watched young birds being pushed off high places by their mothers. Being forced to tumble through the air made them use their wings to save themselves, and in that way their flying began. David knew he must help them, but he tried a gentler method.

Holding each chick carefully, he let it drop. The drop was short, but the stubby wings spread out.

After a few attempts, the Squawks learned to fly a little.

They were also learning to find food for themselves. Still, they liked to have David hand them squids down at the tide pool, and they liked having him give them pieces of fish at the pen.

It was fun. But now meals at the pen required good-sized fish to feed four healthy birds.

CHAPTER 4
Lost in the Fog

One day David decided that he must go deep-sea fishing to get enough food for his sea gulls. He planned to start early the next morning.

That evening the sea was rough at sunset, and the pine trees swished dolefully and beautifully in the wind. Banks of clouds could be seen in the distance, and the air became more moist and chilly. Everyone told David that a storm was coming and that tomorrow morning would be no time to go fishing, not even to get food to feed his seagulls.

David and the Seagulls 37

But at sun-up, the wind had died. The only trouble with the weather was that there was a thick, murky fog.

"Good for fishing," said a Monhegan friend who had come along with David.

David agreed. He was catching fish.

Land was far away, but the fog made it seem farther, almost out of reach.

Even the three large fishing boats nearby were pale shadows in the mist. David wondered how he'd guide his boat back to the island. He listened to the fog horn.

That would be his only guide to the harbor. He heard another sound, a large motorboat coming fast.

Should he turn to avoid being rammed? Should he stop still?

The boat was slowing. David could see it. And it was his father's!

Then came the cheery voice, "Want to be towed? Let's take your fish to the pier."

In another moment, his father threw a towing rope. David caught it and fastened it, and the two fishermen were skimming into port behind the big motorboat. David was content to land. He had his fish.

And the fish were needed. No chance to get food for the gulls along the water's edge now! Not with a violent hurricane whirling up the Atlantic Coast and crashing hard on Monhegan Island! The Coast Guard issued orders for everyone to stay indoors.

The hurricane days were dark.

Then the sun spread a hopeful glow over the waters. A dory was adrift, but most Monhegan boats were safe.

David's boat and his father's weathered the waves where they were moored. David's seagulls, too, were safe.

He knew where they were hiding.

Under the house was the shelter they chose from the gale and the downpour. And they didn't come out until the storm was over.

David and the Seagulls

CHAPTER 5
Saying Goodbye

Vacation days were flying. Soon David must say goodbye to summer, to the island, and to his seagulls.

David and the Seagulls 45

Next summer, his young gulls would be fully grown. David wondered if he would know them. They must be banded.

His friend Jimmie held one of the Squawks in just the right way to have a numbered metal band clamped on his leg. Then came the other Squawk's turn. Finally, Smokey was banded and free to fly away.

But, oh, Orley! He could never fly away. Just the same, he must have a band. It would be a token of friendship.

And blessings came to Orley that very day. One of the lobstermen told David he'd keep the old fellow through the winter, give him warm shelter and plenty of fish.

Everyone loved Orley, the seagull who had managed to make the best of things.

David and the Seagulls 47

The last week of David's vacation came, and then the last day and the last hours. This was goodbye until another summer. But David knew he'd be remembering the island—the sea, the boats, and most of all, his friends, the seagulls.

THE END

Check out these other Level 3 books from The Good and the Beautiful Library!

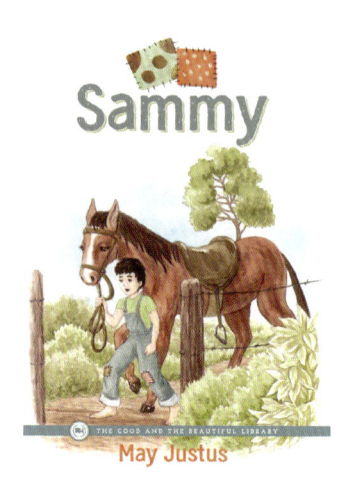

Sammy
By May Justus

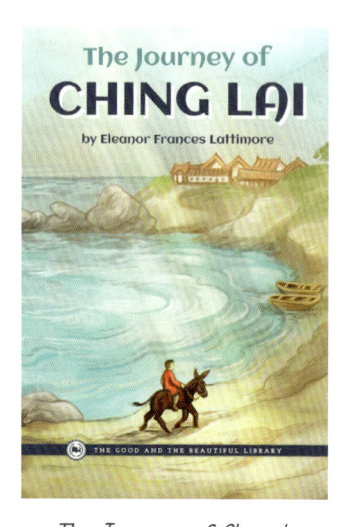

The Journey of Ching Lai
By Eleanor Frances Lattimore

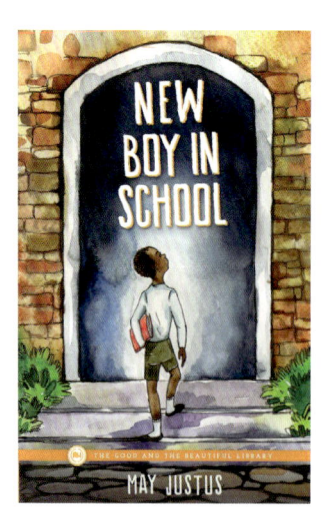

New Boy In School
By May Justus

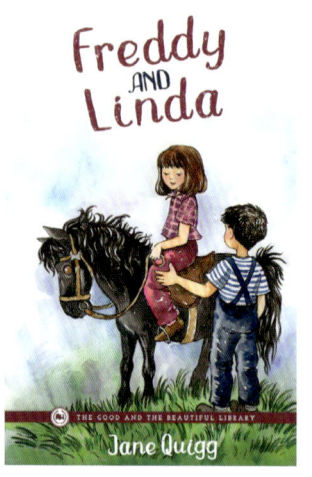

Freddy and Linda
By Jane Quigg